A Jedi
You Will Be

Written by Preeti Chhibber

Illustrated by Mike Deas

Disney
LUCASFILM
PRESS

LOS ANGELES
NEW YORK

For my family, especially the Chhibblings. And "The Child" (aka Baby Yoda). —P. C.

For Annie and Faye —M. D.

For information address Disney · Lucasfilm Press, 1200 Grand Central Avenue, Glendale, California 91201.

Printed in the United States of America

First Edition, October 2020

10 9 8 7 6 5 4 3 2 1

Library of Congress Control Number on file.

FAC-034274-20234

ISBN 978-1-368-05724-0

Visit the official Star Wars website at: www.starwars.com.

Designed by Scott Piehl

DISNEY
LUCASFILM
PRESS

LOS ANGELES
NEW YORK

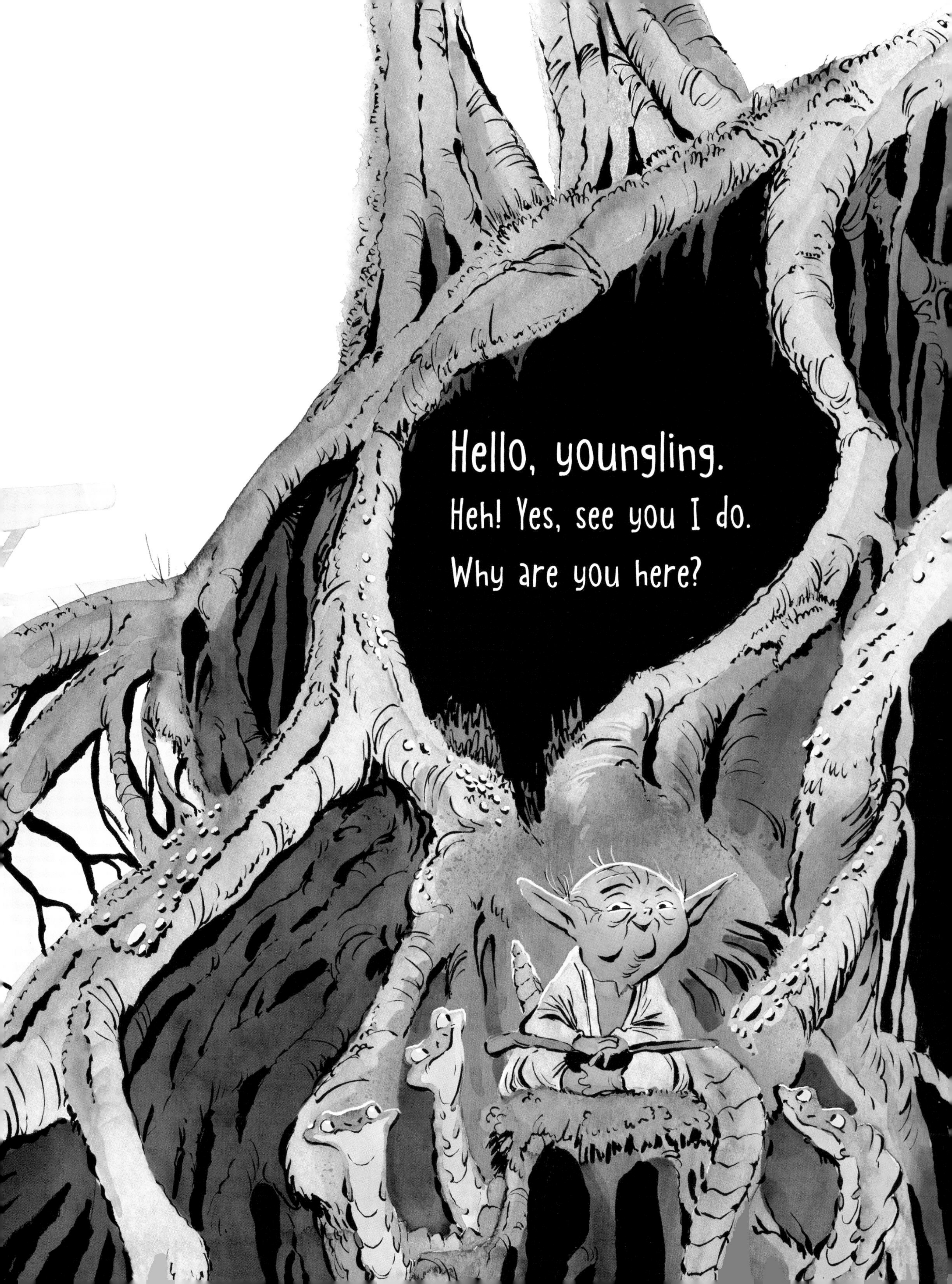
Hello, youngling.
Heh! Yes, see you I do.
Why are you here?

Follow *him*, did you?
Know who that is?

Yes, a great Jedi Luke Skywalker will become.

A Jedi, too, you wish to be?

Help you I can.

Come, come.

Eat first we must.
Strength you will need.
Why a Jedi you wish to be?

Adventure you want?
Excitement you seek?
A Jedi craves not these things.

Ready are you?

What know you of ready?

For eight hundred years have I trained Jedi.

Easy it is not.

A Jedi must have the deepest commitment.

Willing to work hard are you?

Too big are you?

Right you are.
Size matters not.

Finish, will you, what you begin?
Scary things there are. Mean things.
Fear is the path to the dark side.
Fear leads to anger.
Anger leads to hate.
Hate leads to suffering.

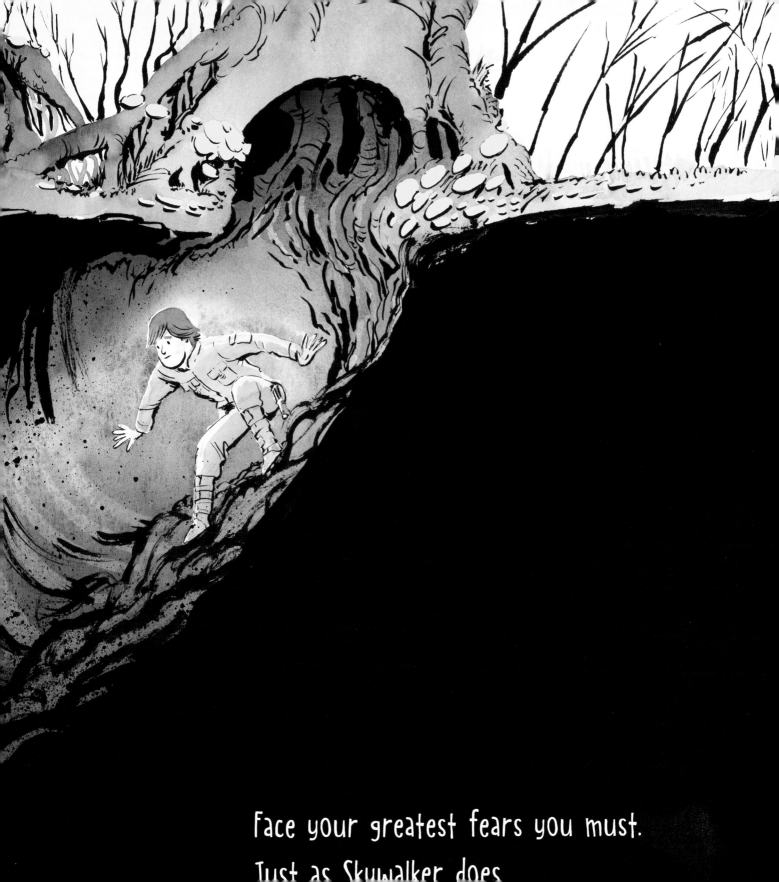

Face your greatest fears you must.
Just as Skywalker does.

Brave can you be?
Calm can you stay?
You will know the good from the bad
when you are at peace.

Now close your eyes.

Closed are they?

See you peeking I do.

Now *breathe*.

Reach out.

A Jedi's strength flows from the Force.

And a powerful ally it is.

Feel it do you?

Life creates it.
Makes it grow.
Its energy surrounds us
and binds us.
You must feel the force around you,
between you and me, the tree, the rock,
everywhere.

A Jedi uses the force for knowledge
and defense, never for attack.
After all, wars not make one great.

And as they seem, things not always are.

Important strength is . . .

...but weakness, too...

...and failure.
Part of the journey they are.

Believe in Skywalker you and I do.
But not yet does Skywalker believe
in himself.

Perhaps together we can
show what is possible.
Reach out.
Feel the Force.
Do or do not.
There is no try.
Do it you *can*.

Before you your path lies.
Hard choices there will be.
Off to face *his* greatest challenge
Skywalker is.
As all Jedi must.

But wiser he will emerge.

As will you, in whatever you may face.

As long as you mind what you have learned...

...a Jedi you will be.

May the Force be with you.